P9-DTU-566

Oh, What a Noisy Farm!

Oh, What a

Harriet Ziefert   pictures by **Emily Bolam**

Noisy Farm!

TAMBOURINE BOOKS NEW YORK

Text copyright © 1995 by Harriet Ziefert
Illustrations copyright © 1995 by Emily Bolam

Library of Congress Cataloging in Publication Data
Ziefert, Harriet. Oh, what a noisy farm! / by Harriet Ziefert ; illustrated by Emily
Bolam. — 1st ed. p. cm. Summary: All the farm animals in this cumulative tale get
into the act when the bull starts chasing the cow around the pasture.
[1. Domestic animals—Fiction. 2. Animal sounds—Fiction.
3. Farm life—Fiction.] I. Bolam, Emily, ill. II. Title.
PZ7.Z4870h 1995 [E]—dc20 94-15171 CIP AC
ISBN 0-688-13260-X (trade). — ISBN 0-688-13261-8 (lib. bdg.)
Printed in Singapore. The text type is Belwe.
1 3 5 7 9 10 8 6 4 2
First edition

Because the bull was chasing the cow,
the farmer's wife shouted,

"Stop, stop, you big, old bull!" and chased
them around the pasture.

When the farmer heard "Stop, stop, you big, old bull!" he grabbed a pot and ran after his wife.

The goat heard "Stop, stop…crash, bang…"
and ran after the farmer and his wife.

The goose heard "Stop, stop…crash, bang…
bleat, bleat…" and ran after the goat, the
farmer, and his wife.

The dog heard "Stop, stop…crash, bang…
bleat, bleat…honk, honk…" and ran after
the goose, the goat, the farmer, and his wife.

The cat heard "Stop, stop…crash, bang…
bleat, bleat…honk, honk…bow wow…"
and ran after the dog, the goose, the goat,
the farmer, and his wife.

With the farmer's wife shouting,
the farmer CRASH BANGING,
the goat BLEAT BLEATING,

the goose HONK HONKING,
the dog BOW WOWING,
and the cat MEOWING—

oh, what a noisy farm!

All of a sudden the cow stopped running.

She turned around and faced the bull.

"Will you be my friend?" the bull asked.

"Yes, I will," mooed the cow.

The farmer said, "Now everyone can take a long nap."

Oh, what a quiet farm!